For Rilynne

She should change her name to OTTER-viano.

A thank-you song to Christy Ottaviano
to be sung to a tune by The Commodores:

(Chorus)
She's a WORD—HOUSE!
Re-write, re-write me, she takes all my bad words out.
She's a WORD—HOUSE!
Her brain is stacked with lots of facts.
She's nice and she has no plaque.

(Bridge)
She knows nouns, she knows nouns, she knows nouns now. *(Repeat)*

* * *

Thanks, Mom, Scott, and Joan, for your
continuous support and encouragement.

SQUARE
FISH

An Imprint of Macmillan

DO UNTO OTTERS. Copyright © 2007 (RESPECTFULLY ON TIME) by Laurie Keller. As PROMISED,
all rights have been CONSIDERATELY reserved. PATIENTLY printed in China by South China Printing
Company Ltd., Dongguan City, Guangdong Province. For information, address Square Fish, 175 Fifth Avenue,
New York, NY 10010.

It's NO LIE, Square Fish and the Square Fish logo are trademarks of Macmillan and are KINDLY used by
Henry Holt and Company under license from Macmillan.
The artist used acrylic paint (which she SHARED with her friends) on Arches watercolor paper to
CARINGLY create the illustrations for this book. NO TEASING took place during the making of this book.
Everyone involved COOPERATED, MADE GOOD EYE CONTACT, and THANKED each other for their hard
work. There was one uncomfortable hair-pulling incident that took place toward the end of this project,
but everyone involved promptly APOLOGIZED and have since FORGIVEN each other.

Library of Congress Cataloging-in-Publication Data
Keller, Laurie.
Do unto otters: a book about manners / Laurie Keller.
p.   cm.
Summary: Mr. Rabbit wonders if he will be able to get along with his new neighbors,
who are otters, until he is reminded of the golden rule.
ISBN 978-0-312-58140-4
[1. Golden rule—Fiction. 2. Neighborliness—Fiction.
3. Rabbits—Fiction. 4. Otters—Fiction.] I. Title.
PZ7.K281346Do 2007   [E]—dc22   2006030505

Originally published in the United States by Christy Ottaviano Books,
an imprint of Henry Holt and Company
Square Fish logo designed by Filomena Tuosto
First Square Fish Edition: September 2009
10 9 8 7 6
macKids.com

F&P: M / LEXILE: AD460L

This book is based on the Golden Rule.

Otts and ENDS

Hi, Hilde!

Do Unto Otters

(A Book About Manners)

By

Laurie Keller

SQUARE FISH

Henry Holt and Company
New York

DOO-DEE-DOO

DOO-
DEE-
DOO

back home

OTTERS?

OTTERS?

My new neighbors are

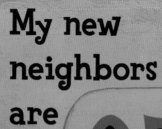

OTTERS!

I don't know anything about <u>otters</u>.
What if we don't get along?

Mr. Rabbit, I know an old saying:

"DO UNTO OTTERS AS YOU WOULD HAVE OTTERS DO UNTO YOU."

What does **THAT** mean?

It simply means treat otters the same way you'd like otters to treat you.

Treat otters the same way I'd like otters to treat me?

Hmmm...

How would I like otters to treat me?

How would I ...

... like OTTERS ...

...to treat ME?

Well . . . I'd like otters to be FRIENDLY.

A cheerful hello,

a nice smile,

and good eye contact

are all part of being friendly.

Friendliness is very important to me—especially after my last neighbor, Mrs. Grrrrrrr.

I'd like otters to be POLITE.

They should Know when to say

"PLEASE"

PLEASE LOOK (:

They should Know when to say

"THANK YOU."

THANKS FOR LOOKING! C:

And they should Know when to say

"EXCUSE ME."

EXCUSE ME! BURP

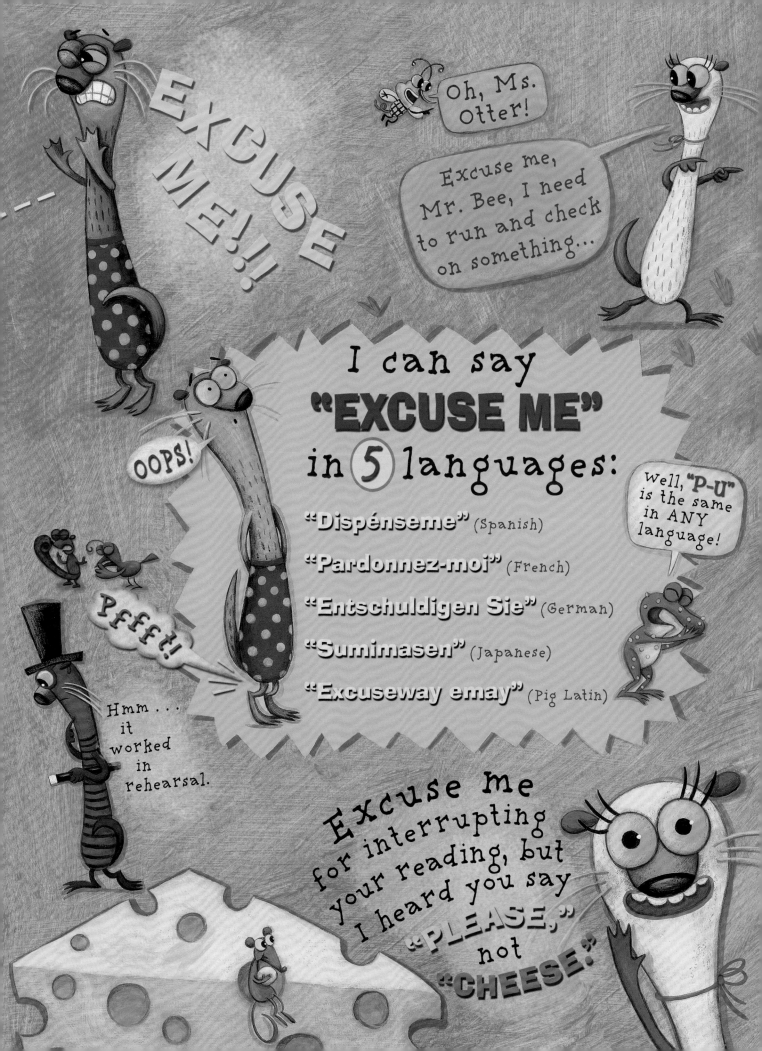

Otters should be

HONEST.

That means they should

KEEP THEIR PROMISES

My word is as good as GOLD (fish)!

NOT LIE

I never lie— it makes my whiskers itch.

NOT CHEAT

Cheating makes my whiskers itch, too. . . . I wonder if I should see a doctor?

I'd like otters to be CONSIDERATE.

You know...

BEING A GOOD LISTENER

ASKING BEFORE BORROWING SOMETHING

NOT LITTERING

BEING PATIENT

CARING FOR ALL CREATURES
(big and small)

OPENING THE DOOR FOR SOMEONE

BEING ON TIME

RESPECTING THE ELDERLY

HELPING NEIGHBOR UNTANGLE EARS

It's always good to have a considerate neighbor.

It wouldn't hurt otters to be KIND.

(Everyone appreciates a kind act
no matter how bad it smells.)

Oh, and what's that word?...

"COOPERATE!"

Otters should learn to cooperate.

Did someone say "OPERATE"?

CO-operate: to work well together

We know how to co-OTTER-ate!

I see otters
like to play.

Wheeeeeee!

I'd like it if we could SHARE things:

our favorite books,

Harry Otter

Goldilocks and the Three Hares

our favorite activities,

our favorite treats

(hmmm . . . maybe not the treats).

I hope otters WON'T TEASE me about:

My "Doo-Dee-Doo" song

My extra-large swim fins

My "bad hare days"

I hope otters won't tease ANYONE about ANYTHING.

I think otters should **APOLOGIZE** when they do something wrong.

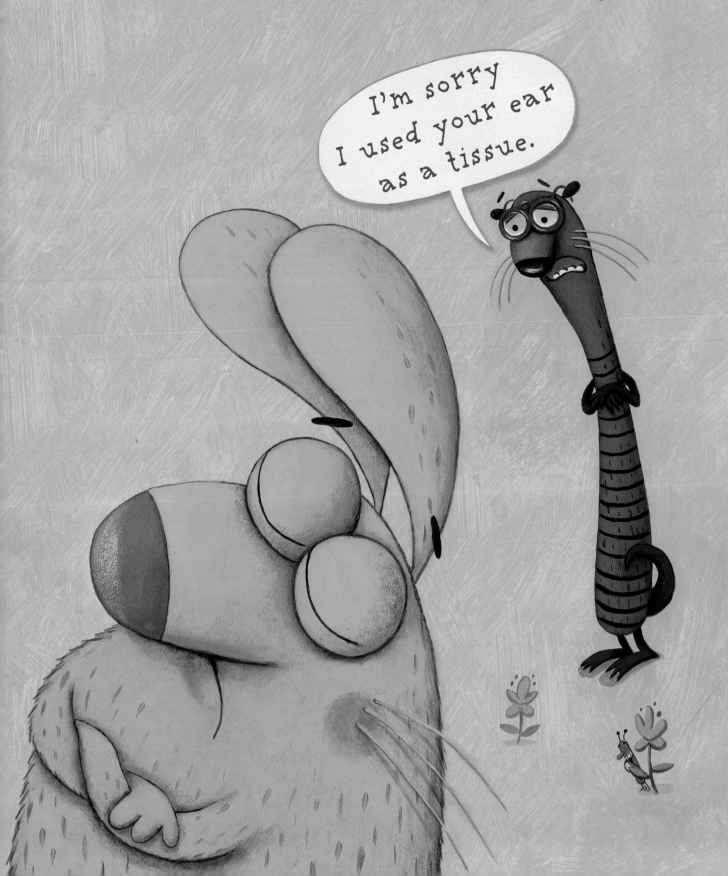

And I hope they can be **FORGIVING** when I do something wrong.

So there.
That's how I'd
like otters to
treat me.

You see,
Mr. Rabbit,
I told you it
was simple!

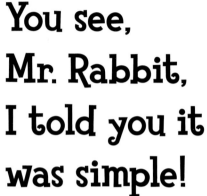